RUPERT CROWN

RUPERT CROWN

by

ROB BROWN

authorHOUSE®

AuthorHouse™ UK Ltd.
1663 Liberty Drive
Bloomington, IN 47403 USA
www.authorhouse.co.uk
Phone: 0800.197.4150

© 2013 by Rob Brown. All rights reserved.

No part of this book may be reproduced, stored in a retrieval system, or transmitted by any means without the written permission of the author.

Published by AuthorHouse   10/04/2013

ISBN: 978-1-4817-6962-4 (sc)
ISBN: 978-1-4817-7020-0 (e)

Any people depicted in stock imagery provided by Thinkstock are models, and such images are being used for illustrative purposes only. Certain stock imagery © Thinkstock.

This book is printed on acid-free paper.

Because of the dynamic nature of the Internet, any web addresses or links contained in this book may have changed since publication and may no longer be valid. The views expressed in this work are solely those of the author and do not necessarily reflect the views of the publisher, and the publisher hereby disclaims any responsibility for them.

*My thanks to Patricia Lacy
for her proof reading and helpful advice*

Work hard

"Work hard," his mother had said. She meant well. She wanted the best for her Rupert; the apple of her eye, her mummy's boy, but what was it that she wanted for him? *She* worked hard; poking at the washing in the gas copper outside the back door. The copper took up so much room, you had to squeeze past it to get to the outside lavatory. They had two lavatories; one outside under the covered way, next to the coalhouse, and another one upstairs in the bathroom. Auntie Ada and Auntie Renie and Auntie Vi only had one. Auntie Renie's wasn't even near the house. It was at the bottom of the garden. He didn't like to go to the lavatory at Auntie Renie's, it had a funny smell. His outside lavatory smelled a bit like that, but it wasn't as bad. There was always a gnat on the wall; sometimes two. He would sometimes peer closely at them for quite a long time; strange, wispy things. Two of their hair-like legs trailed up behind them as they clung onto the wall. If you looked really closely, you could see a pointed thing on the head. That's what they got you with. If you were quick, you could squash one on the wall, but it made a red mark on the wall when you did, and, when his mother saw the red marks, she was not very pleased. Christian Price, who was a year younger than Rupert and lived next door, said that the red was the blood of people it had been feeding from. Christian was very interested in biology and had a pond in his garden with great crested newts. When a gnat got you, it would come up in a red bump and it would itch. If you scratched it, it got worse but, if you bit your teeth together hard, and didn't scratch it, you could stop it hurting. It was the same with stinging nettles. His mother always said: "Lick a dock leaf and put on it." He tried that but it was not as good as biting hard and trying to ignore it.

"Yes," he had answered. But, what was it to work hard. Working hard was doing things you didn't want to do. At school, and for that matter, at home as well, he had always been keen on nature study and art and science and making things, but there were lots of things he didn't want to do. If you bit hard, sometimes you could do them well enough but, sometimes, it really was *very* hard. In the winter, when his mother washed the clothes, her hands got red and cracked. She laughed and put Vaseline on them. His father would look at them and say: "Oh, Gaud," and then turn the page of the Daily Mirror. They took the Daily Mirror on week-days and Saturday and the Sunday Pictorial on Sundays. Sometimes, in the Sunday Pictorial, there would be a lady without her top clothes on. He sometimes saw his mother without her top clothes on. At school you had to have all your clothes off when you ran through the showers after PT and Games. He didn't like that. It made him feel funny and he would be as quick as possible. Philip Lucas took ages in the showers. He would dance around and show off.

"Come 'ome straight away fo' yer dinner."

"Yes," he had said as he wandered off towards the grammar school at the top of the road. Both his parents had been very pleased when he passed the scholarship. His mother had beamed all over her face and said: "Up the Crowns." He had been sent off on his bike on the first Saturday morning to tell all his aunts and uncles; who gave him money. Uncle Tim gave him half a crown. Uncle Tim was his dad's brother. He had said: "Half a crown for a Crown," and seemed very pleased with what he had said. Auntie Ada and Auntie Vi gave him two shillings and Auntie Renie only gave him one and sixpence. Uncle Tim was on his dad's side and Auntie Ada,

Auntie Vi and Auntie Renie were on his mother's side.

At the council school, all the kids had stood lined up in the playground while the headmaster, Mr. Cranley, read out the names of the ones who had passed. He started with Jennifer Allen. Her name always came first. *His* name was always number four on the school lists. "John Ardern, well done John," went on Mr. Cranley. He strained on tip-toe to look over the five heads in front of him towards the grey-tufted, balding despot reading the list. When he heard the next name, Jimmy Doplin, his heart sank. What would his mum and dad say. Doplin comes after Crown and Crown had not been called out. Mr. Cranley carried on down the list and he listened so carefully to see if his name had somehow got out of order but he didn't hear it. He felt funny in his stomach and he wanted to go to the lavatory. Ron Jinks had had his name called. Ron was his second cousin and they went to Sunday school together. After Sunday school, on alternate weeks, Ron would come to Rupert's house for tea or Rupert would go to Ron's and they would play at this and that for an hour or so afterwards. Ron would be going to the grammar school. It had looked as though Mr. Cranley had got to the bottom of the list, because he shuffled the papers and started to fold them but, as he did so he looked up and, with a grin across to

Miss Blanchard, slowly said: "And finally, Rupert Crown." He was startled and didn't know if he had heard correctly. Why had Mr. Cranley not read his name out in the usual place if it was on the list. He couldn't understand. Mr. Cranley had walked away and the disciplined ranks of children had dissolved into a chattering mass. He had pushed through towards Miss Blanchard, his class teacher, and had asked: "Have I passed Miss?"

"Typical, Rupert Crown. Your ears were never your strong point, were they! Yes, it seems you have." Miss Blanchard hadn't seemed particularly pleased. She almost seemed cross.

Just before the summer holidays started, all the kids had what was called a preliminary visit to the schools they would be going to, the next term. He already knew something about the grammar school because, several times in the past, he had been to their annual sports day which was always held on a summer Saturday and was a big event in the town. Also, Ron lived on Davenport Road, which ran from Smuts lane to Baxter Road and so, his garden backed onto the main school playing field which was on the same site as all the main school buildings. The field had a long jump pit, a high jump pit, tennis courts and a cricket square. You could easily get through Ron's bottom fence there and they used to play cricket and football on it in the light evenings, or at holiday times, when all was quiet. They never played on the actual cricket square itself, just well away at the edge, although the ball would sometimes go as far as the square if Ron played one of his master strokes. They would often be joined by John Boulder, who was the son of the grammar school caretaker. They would also sometimes play 'commandos' around the school grounds and particularly in the school shrubbery. John was a year older but went to the secondary modern school at the other end of the town. Rupert never knew why it was called 'modern'; and the grammar school was apparently not 'modern'.

Anyway, this was the main part of the grammar school, but there were two other parts. There were other playing fields, about half a mile away, along Baxter Road and, about a quarter of a mile away, along Smuts Lane was Hill View where there were art rooms in the old house, and a metalwork room. From the large windows of the art rooms, you could see for a very long way over Bell's Wood and the Leicestershire countryside. Rupert thought what a very good name 'Hill View' was. Also at Hill View, in the large garden, there was a circular pond. Christian's dad was a teacher at the grammar school and Rupert would sometimes go with Christian to fish in the pond there; that was where he got his great crested newts.

Rupert's mother had taken him shopping for his new school uniform, which was a black blazer and grey, long trousers, and his games kit and the real leather satchel. The games shirts had to have yellow because he was in Priory house. The houses were Fosse, Watling, Priory and Castle. They were all names of Roman roads. Mr. Rodham, his new headmaster, said they were roads to all their futures. There had to be a badge for the blazer pocket. On the badge was some writing: 'Deum Timeto Regem Honorato'. It meant 'Fear God and Honour the King' and it was Latin. It was called the school motto. He wasn't quite sure what it meant. The motto was carved in big letters above the stage in the big hall. You didn't go into the big hall very often whilst you were a junior because the juniors had morning assembly in the gym. You weren't allowed to wear your outdoor shoes in the gym because the polished wooden floor had to be kept shiny. So, everybody had to sit cross-legged on the shiny floor holding their shoes. The boys sat on the left and the girls sat on the right and Miss Pollack would sweep in down the central gangway. She was in charge and all the form teachers of the first and second years would sit on chairs down the sides. Sometimes, because of the way the girls sat, you could get a glimpse of their knickers without them realising that they were on show. He thought that Maggie Driffil enjoyed showing her knickers but he would not have liked her to catch him looking at them. She was in his form and the first time he spoke to her, she dug her nails into the back of his hand so hard that it left blue marks for quite a long time. He didn't know why she had done that because he was only trying to be friendly. He was often puzzled by how other kids could be and it scared him.

About a month ago he had been dared to eat his apple during assembly. Everybody had looked at him and so he had agreed. He was seen by Miss Boxill. She taught Latin. Her ginger hair was a tight plaited knot and she was round-shouldered. She reminded him of a vulture; the black wings of her gown hanging from her. She was very cross and had given him the task of writing out the hymn and the prayer for that morning as a punishment. Mr. Thomas had said that if he had caught him he would have taken him straight to the headmaster. The hymn was easy enough, because everybody had a hymn book, but the prayer was a different matter and proved not at all simple to get hold of. He was taken by surprise, later that same day, to come face to face with Miss Boxill as they rounded a corner of one of the buildings. It had been a kind of cover for nervousness that made him say: "When do you want that work Miss?" She had bristled immediately saying that that was 'rank insolence' and that he could now write it all out twice! He was not sure what 'insolence' was but he could not understand why Miss Boxill should have been so cross.

He had been put into 1B. The forms were labelled 1A, 1B, 1C and 1D. 1A was the top form; Ron Jinks and Jennifer Allen were in 1A. He only knew a few of the kids in his form; the ones who had been at the council school. Mrs. Hood was his form teacher. She was nice. She was kind of soft and warm like his mother. She slipped on the ice in the quadrangle as she was walking to the new block which was where the first year classrooms were. He was there because he was waiting outside for her. He didn't much care for the idle moments in class when teachers were not there. She had seemed very embarrassed. She must have thought that he would laugh but he thought that she might have hurt herself. He had picked up the papers she dropped. Teachers always expect pupils to laugh if they have an accident.

There were thirty five pupils in his class. Three other boys had the same surname as him but they were not related. Alan had ginger hair and freckles. He was always talking about 'diabetic'. He had to have an injection every day.

Sometimes he came over all funny and had to have a biscuit. Ian was all right. *He* was third and then there was Steve. You had to be a bit careful of Steve. Last week in Biology, some of the others said he put his hand inside Maggie Driffil's knickers.

He arrived at the first entrance and went through and round to the right towards the quad outside the new block. There were four classrooms in the block, two on the ground floor and two upstairs. His was upstairs and, because a teacher outside on the quad could not see in, was more isolated than the ones downstairs. It was a chilly morning and so it would be natural to go straight inside. There were not in fact many outside and so the dilemma was to be exposed without the protection of the presence of a teacher inside upstairs or to be safe but isolated outside where he might be exposed to taunts of: "What yer scared of Crownie?" He steeled himself and made his way up into the classroom. He went straight to his desk, eyes front, and asked Ian if he had managed to do the English homework. Surreptitiously he took in the wider scene. All the usual potential was there but it seemed for the moment to be contained. Mrs. Hood arrived, the first relief, and there would be no gap for a while because she would be taking maths first period after registration.

The maths lesson had got well underway. He had been shown how to do HCFs and LCMs but he wasn't absolutely sure what they were actually for. The class had been set some exercises and Mrs. Hood sat at her desk at the front; deeply engrossed in some marking. This pre-occupation together with the mild paper rustling of a more or less purposeful atmosphere was enough to mask the effect of the odd paper pellet flicked by a rubber band. Maggie Driffil, the girl who was casting a lengthening shadow over Rupert's life was involved and he felt he had to grin approvingly a couple of times, although had only thin faith in ensuring immunity from her taunts by appearing to join ranks. Odd how he felt he had to give this attention for safety's sake.

"Crown R., you can square forty-eight and prove it by subtraction. I'm getting a little tired of your lack of diligence." The others had been sharp enough to avoid notice but he had walked straight into the trap. Caught again. Mrs. Hood was nice but she did not really understand. He did not want to annoy her but he had to try to do something to ensure peace during the testing times.

Maths had finished and Mr. Thomas, the geography teacher was late. Maggie Driffil was fooling around with some of the boys just a couple of rows of desks away and, every so often, laughing coarsely. Boredom was growing into an evil monster with every passing minute of delay. She teased one of the boys and then looked around. Rupert tried to become inconspicuous but, like trying to run faster in a bad dream, it was having the opposite effect. He knew that, if the teacher did not come, it would be certain that she would start on him. He sensed the evil restlessness in the air. He did not wish to hurt anyone else just because there was nothing else to do so why should anyone else behave like that. And, why should he be afraid. But he was afraid; more and more uncomfortable by the minute. Pulse beginning to race and sweating under his arms and between his legs. Her eyes met his. The noise of the class was mounting. She left the group she had exhausted her jibes on for the moment and was coming over. She began talking to Lucy Smith who had the desk immediately to the left of Rupert. Lucy was not quite one of the coarse crowd and she was, to some extent, handling herself on a tight-rope too but coping well enough. He felt most uncomfortable now with the threat of ridicule and humiliation again so close. All at once, she turned and looked straight at him so that the confrontation, which he dreaded, now faced him directly. How should he react?

A few of the others had turned their attention in his direction; eager for some fresh sport;

there being nothing else to do. William Harris, a stocky, strong boy, grinned challengingly across at him. Harris had grabbed him round the neck from behind and pulled him under the last time they were at the baths. He had sat on the side for minutes coughing and trying to get his breath back but none of the teachers seemed to notice. All that happened eventually was that Mr. Steel had told him to stop messing about and get on with his lengths.

After about a full half minute, the girl picked up the metal top of Rupert's pen, dropped it onto the floor and then stamped on it, flattening it. Rupert began to tremble. How could anyone hurt someone else completely without conscience? He was amazed and frightened. How to react. All eyes were on him now. Under her mocking grin, he could feel the tears welling up inside him. He bit hard but it was really very hard to control the emotion and he longed for the relief of just letting go. But he would be nothing if he did. Why him? She wouldn't do it to anybody else. He did not know what to do and worse than that, he had hesitated. He was on stage and on trial before the whole class. He felt the condemnation of everybody for his weakness. He was a nothing, a nobody, a weak, frail figure of fun and that was it. His sensitive heart cried out within him as his lower lip quivered uncontrollably. 'Why me, why me?

There are others who would not know what to do but she doesn't pick on them. Why me?'

"Crownie's crying," she called back to the others as she reached out and pushed him in the chest. He just might have pushed back if it had been a boy but you shouldn't push girls like that.

"Stop that," he called out without a great deal of commitment.

"Oh-er, stop that," she mimicked, "I'm scared." Now she reached out to cuff him one around the head. He flinched away and she missed. Just as she was about to have a more determined go, measured steps could be heard coming up the stairs. There was a well-practised swift scurrying and, when Mr. Thomas came through the doorway, it was upon a scene of well ordered calm.

Auntie Ada

Some Geography was interesting but the coalfields of the midlands were not interesting enough to stop him thinking of Maggie Driffil. His writing had gone all spidery because he could not stop the tremor in his hand. He stopped writing, put down his pen and tried to relax the hand on the desk for a moment. "Stop slacking and get on Crown R!" came the dispassionate directive from Mr. Thomas. Why did teachers always look across at him at the wrong moment? He continued to scratch along the lines of the exercise book until the break-time bell.

At break-time, it was not too bad because it was always possible to go where there was a teacher or a prefect on duty. There was the tuck shop run by Mr. Boulder, the school caretaker and there was free milk in the quadrangle. Because some did not take their milk at all, there was always plenty spare, and if the big kids did not get there first, you could get extras. The prefects had black blazers too but they had red all around the edge and along the lapels and along the pockets. It was called red braid. They had caps too but they had a red tassel hanging from the little button on the top. You had to do what prefects said, just like teachers but sometimes prefects would swear at you. He never heard teachers swear like that even when they got very cross. He usually had to go to the toilets in the quadrangle at break-time and nearly always there would be prefects there smoking cigarettes.

After break it was Metalwork at Hill View. He liked going there, both for the Metalwork and for Art in the old house. From the paths and the art room windows there really was a nice view of the woods and the common where he and Christian had adventures and you could see almost to Leicester in the distance. He liked both subjects and he even went there to special art club in the old house on Saturday mornings. He really liked making things though and today he would be using the forge again; heating the iron rod to red hot and bashing it with the heavy hammer on the anvil. He was making a spade scraper. He enjoyed using the machines too and he would need to drill holes for rivets. There were two lathes and two drilling machines. He found it quite straightforward to cut down a line with a hacksaw while most of the other kids found it difficult. Mr. Bearford taught him Metalwork. The kids called him 'basher' Bearford. Rupert never saw him bash anybody but he thought he was quite fierce and just might if he was provoked enough. Maggie Driffil would be doing Domestic Science in the main school and miles away.

As they walked along Smuts Lane, they were passed by Miss Pollack on her moped. She taught Art at Hill View and would be there in plenty of time to receive her class. Miss Pollack seemed ever so old and had taught his dad when he had gone to the grammar school. Basher Bearford seemed to spend just about all his time at Hill View and you hardly ever saw him travelling to and fro. Basher caught 'Pongo' Sieley messing about in Metalwork the week before, and he got so cross with him that hardly anybody spoke again for the rest of the lesson and there was just the noise of the tools and the vices.

Rupert went home for dinner and his house was near the top of Meadow Road off Smuts Lane so it was just about the same distance as going back to main school. His sister was called Fran and was three and a half years younger than he and was still at the council school. She was already sitting at the table when he got in and his mother was busy in the kitchen.

"Sit down quick Rupert," his mother called, almost monotone, as she noticed him, "yer dad'll be 'ere in a minit."

He moved over to the table and then there was the sound of the Standard Eight pulling onto the drive. His mother was down the hallway to open the door and his dad came in. They were soon into the sausage and mashed potato. His mother seemed less lively than usual; almost quiet, then said to his dad: "Ada's 'ad them tests again. I *shall* be glad when she's over all this."

"It's no good goin' on like that Marge," his dad came back almost cross, "she's not goin' to get over it." This caused a pause and a tear rolled down his mother's cheek and hung off the end of her chin. "She's not goin' to get over it," more gently now, perhaps realising that his first response had been too abrupt. It seemed to Rupert that his dad often got cross and as often as not it was *him* he got cross with; never did he get cross with his sister Fran. He kept quiet and carried on with his dinner. The elder son and the younger daughter. Entirely different species. The one has to earn his respect whilst the other is to be protected.

"Is Auntie Ada really poorly Daddy?" asked Fran.

"Well, she's had this problem darlin' but the doctors 're doin' what they can. P'raps she'll be all right."

Auntie Ada was the eldest of his mother's sisters but she had married, who was now his Uncle John, only two years ago. Uncle John's first wife had died of exactly the same thing as Auntie Ada had now; Rupert had pieced together, from snippets of remarks from his mum and dad and from his other aunts. She had had a 'growth' removed in an operation and she now had a 'bag'.

He had called in to see Auntie Ada with his mum and Auntie Vi only the week before.

"'Ow yer feelin' now then Ada?" his mum had asked.

"Oh, I think om a bit better today," she had replied, but her words were slurred. She lay, propped up on several pillows, in the single bed which had been set up for her in the downstairs living room for some time now. "'ello me duck," she offered to Rupert with a pitying, almost apologetic tone of voice. Her arms, very thin and veiny, lay lifeless on top of the counterpane. It seemed to Rupert, that she was almost saying: 'Look at me, what a state I'm in, aren't I'.

The sisters had rambled on as they always did and Rupert almost admired the way they found so many words to say so little. Occasional gestures however, underlined that this gathering was not quite the same as usual. At one point, Auntie Ada, became a little more conscious of herself and lifted the boney stick of her right arm and looked at it as though to say: 'does this thing really belong to me?' She was helped to drink tea and the sound of the liquid going down was rather like that of water down a drainpipe. How was this frail, hollow, human being still alive? It made Rupert very sad to see her like this.

His dad worked at a hosiery factory on the other side of the town. He was a department manager. He always came home for dinner at half past twelve. Rupert was glad that the grammar school was just up the road because that meant that he did not have to stay for school dinners and could get away from the other kids for a while and, in any case, he was not sure he would like the food. Today, after the sausage and mash, it would be apple pie and custard. Almost whenever they had custard, his dad would ask: "Is it Auntie Polly custard?" This was because once, when Auntie Polly had come to stay, his dad thought the custard was better than usual and that his mum had made a special effort for Auntie Polly. His dad would grin as he said it and obviously thought it was quite witty. There was no such teasing today however, and the meal passed under a kind of strained silence.

Rupert finished eating and asked: "Please may I leave the table?"

"Wait a minit, yer dad's not finished 'is dinner yet," his mother replied. His father always took ages to eat his food. Rupert sank back on his chair and reacted as impassively as he could to his father's disapproving look. Eventually, and it certainly seemed long enough, he was up and about to head for the back door and the garden. "Bring yer pots in the kitchen Rupert," his mother said, rather obviously; further disapproval on the face of his father. At last he was away down the garden to the shed but accompanied by the maternal message: "Don't be too long down there Rupert or you'll be late getting' back t' school!"

"No, I'm just doing a bit in the shed."

"Well I don't want to 'ave to come an' get yer."

"All right." He went into the shed. It was a good shed. It wasn't a bought one; his dad and he had made it; well, his dad had really made it; but he had helped; and helped quite a lot. They had made it from new wood; not out of packing cases, which his dad sometimes got from the factory. It was eight feet by fourteen feet with a pitched roof. It was covered in asbestos sheets on the walls and roofing felt on the roof. It had a bench with a big, Record, woodwork vice and his dad's tools were all around and hanging on the walls. He approached the bench, picked up the rasp and continued working the piece of wood which was gripped in the vice and which, ever so slowly was turning into a miniature cricket bat. Mini-cricket was becoming something of a latest fad at school, with barely adequate improvisations, such as someone's geometry set box as a bat and someone else's for the wicket, and a tennis ball as a very much out of scale object. Rupert had spotted the niche and expected, quite soon, to improve the situation. He was sure that it would be better if they could use a proper, scaled down bat and, who knows, proper stumps as well.

His mother was not at all pleased to have to come all the way down the garden: "You are a nuisance Rupert. It's nearly ten to two. You'll be late." Without a watch, he had simply become lost in his current passion. He dropped the tool onto the bench and ran.

He got into the classroom, out of breath and just before Mrs Hood called his name for registration. However, this did not save him from a stern: "You are supposed to be *in* this room by two o'clock Crown R!"

Bell's Wood

Weekends were good; Maggie Driffil was a million miles away and Rupert was pleased with his pen and ink of the countryside from the art room window. He was beginning to colour wash it, using the paint box he had received as a Christmas present from Uncle Tim. He was becoming something of a leading light at the Saturday morning art club at Hill View. Ironically, possibly his greatest compliment came from Maggie Driffil herself, who, on seeing one of his efforts, sneered: "You din't do that Crownie!" This, of course, was aside from making further progress on the miniature cricket bat and stumps which were coming along nicely. The miniature cricket craze at school was still in full swing and the kids were still using such as a hymn book for a bat and an up-turned geometry set tin for a wicket.

The same, late Spring, Saturday, early afternoon, was warm and fine. Rupert and Christian

Price had decided on a trip to the woods and particularly to the brook that ran around Bell's Wood. Christian had a shrimping net from his last seaside holiday whilst Rupert had made a net from one of his mother's old stockings, a bit of wire and a length of bamboo cane he had found in the garden. They each got geared up, tying a string 'handle' onto an empty jam jar, and set off. Down the road, right at the bottom and left over the blue-brick railway bridge, which spanned a fairly steep-sided cutting. Always pause here and look over the side; seemed pretty quiet today. Then, on left, down the rough lane and alongside the railway line. Quite soon, the lane was on a level with the line and there was a pair of steps, one over each hedge at opposite sides of the tracks for pedestrians to cross. Here, the two climbed over. Here, if you bent right down and put your ear to a rail, you could hear if a train was approaching far off. Here, if you put a penny on the line and a train did come, it flattened it right out as big as a saucer. Still nothing yet today. They moved on, where the railway was now up on an embankment. Large areas of the grass of the embankment had been burnt black where a recent passing train had emptied ashes from its firebox. They went past 'The Spinney', and into the first field, and then the second, before the common. This was part of Bell's Farm and the footpath went close to the farm house which had a couple of benches with seats in the front garden, where you could buy a bottle of Tizer or Vimto. On this occasion, spare cash was the problem. They just might have enough for an ice cream at Cramp's shop on the way back, and so the two passed by and around onto the common. The favoured location was in one corner alongside the wood where the brook widened and deepened just enough to offer good prospects. Each quietly took up a position and peered into the clear, swiftly moving water.

"There's one," said Rupert immediately, "and another; sticklebacks."

"Yes, it's looking good," replied Christian.

They each, half filled their jam jar, and started dipping their net into the stream but the darting little creatures were pretty good at evading capture and it was quite some time before one had a turn of bad luck. "Got one!" called out Christian excitedly and he quickly conveyed his catch to his jam jar. "It's a male. Look at the red on it." They both examined it minutely, still darting vigorously, exploring its new situation; so abruptly thrust upon it. It was captive, imprisoned, vulnerable. To the two boys however, it was just a prize and a reward for their patience.

After a couple of hours, Rupert had overtaken his friend by one stickleback but then, in an exciting final round, Christian had bagged a bullhead. "What a magnificent specimen," he declared and, certainly, Rupert was quite envious.

"Are you going to put 'em in your pond?" enquired Rupert.

"Definitely, I've been after a bullhead, particularly, for a while."

"I think I'll put mine back 'cos I haven't really got a proper place for 'em."

"I could take yours as well if you like, and you can always come round to see them."

"OK. I'll carry 'em back then."

They were ready to call it a day and were getting things together when there was a call from the wood: "We c'n see yer Crownie!" It had been pretty quiet apart from every now and then a slight wind rustling the tree tops, the occasional bird song, the gentle tinkling of the flowing stream, and, in all, just four trains had passed. In all this time, nobody had passed by at all. Although they had been well occupied for most of the time, whenever they had looked around, across the common, there had been nobody at all in sight. The call was coarse and threatening. It was a kid's voice but it was immediately unnerving. The two boys reacted, and looked, firstly in the direction from which it had appeared to come, and then at each other, and then back to the wood again. Each was caught by surprise; shock even. Rupert's reaction quickly developed further; the familiar feeling in his stomach; a strange apprehension. "We c'n still see yer Crownie!" it came again and this time, it was followed by laughter; of what seemed like more than one person. It had come from a slightly different direction and, as they now concentrated, they could just make out the occasional rustle of undergrowth.

"Who do you think they are?" asked Christian.

"Dunno," replied Rupert, "but we've finished here haven't we? Let's go."

"A' yer runnin' away Crownie?" came the continuing taunt from the mask of leaves. "What yer scared of?"

Rather than take the easier option footpath alongside the wood, the two waded through the knee-deep grasses of the field which enabled them more quickly to put a distance between them and their covert adversaries; the coarse, taunting voices diminishing. For Rupert, there was a strange vulnerability in the open space of the field; no protection and a great relief, slightly out of breath, to reach the gate at the far side. From the other side of the gate, time to take stock, to look back; but on a completely peaceful scene. No movement at all. They lingered for quite some time; staring across the void of varied green. Then, one by one, three distant figures emerged from the wood, way over to the right, much too far away for the two to be able to recognise them, if indeed they might have been recognisable anyway. But, they *did* know Rupert's name, so who were they? Surely they would be from school and, how would he feel back at school, suspicious of every perceived malicious grin. Would this be yet another threat to his already fragile self esteem? Anyway, this day's curious threat was now over and they were safe. They watched until the tiny dots had disappeared around a rise in the land and then turned towards home. At the railway bridge, instead of crossing immediately, they decided to go on the hundred yards or so to Cramp's shop at the end of the lane where it met Station Road. They were quite relaxed again by now and were in no hurry at all but, gradually aware of footsteps behind them, turned to see two older boys walking briskly in the same direction and nearly level with them. Christian appeared completely unconcerned but Rupert experienced a slight anxiety for a second or two. Perhaps it was because of what had happened earlier, but also, although it was not far to the shop, the lane here had a thick, tall hedge along the left and the deep railway cutting was along the right, and so it was in fact quite secluded at the mid-point, which is where they now were. The feeling passed as the older boys overtook them, walking on the left hand side of the lane, and, without a word, just carried on. Safe again. But, about fifteen yards ahead of them, the two older boys, as though they were performing a rehearsed routine, wheeled around and casually wandered back towards them. They were not just returning to where they had come from because Rupert and Christian were close to the wire fence on the railway side and these two characters were definitely heading straight towards them. The younger boys instinctively stopped first and the older boys slowed as they approached until they too stopped but as close as about a yard away. They were kind of rough looking, one fair-haired and one dark. Each had a couple of tears in his shirt and mucky, long trousers. They were close enough for Rupert to notice the smell that some of the poor kids at the council school used to have. The fair-haired one was taller and stockier and was smiling broadly; the other was just sort of looking on. There was something about the smile though; something not quite right. "What yer got there then?" the taller lad opened with a not quite genuine friendliness, "sticklebacks ar' the'?"

"Yes," said Christian, "and a bullhead."

"Oh, a bull'ead," replied the other in what was now plainly a mocking approval as he turned to his companion and they both sniggered to each other. "Let's 'ave a look then." He reached out for the jar and Christian, who was beginning to look quite scared, offered no serious resistance and let the jar slip from his hand. "Jus' look at 'em Jim, swimmin' little buggers; 'ere you 'old 'em fer a bit but mind yer dump drop 'em." Jim took the jar, grinned broadly and, feigning clumsiness, caused a slosh of water to fall to the ground. One stickleback had also fallen and Rupert immediately bent down to rescue its silver, sparkling, wriggling body and popped it into his own jar.

"That's very clever mate," Jim spoke for the first time, "y've saved 'im, aint 'e Bill."

"Yea, clever, that," said Bill, and turning to Rupert said: "put yer jar down. 'Ave yer ever 'ad a chinese burn?"

For Rupert, this was after all one of those dead end situations; no way out. These two were too big to fight and probably too big to out run. All the familiar feelings of persecution were welling up in him. Why was this happening to him? Why were these two bullies so unfeeling? "I don't know," he said trying not to let the quiver in his lip show, "what do you mean?"

"I'll show yer," said Bill, "roll yer sleeve up."

Rupert knew no other than to obey and Bill gripped his fore-arm tight with both hands close together and then twisted in opposite directions.

"'Urts don' it," sniggered Jim.

"Yes," replied Rupert wincing at the pain and looking at the red wheel developing around his arm.

"Right," said Bill to Rupert, "tek yer shoes off."

A not very convincing: "Why," was the only surprised reaction Rupert could muster.

"Becos' I'll beat yer up if yer don't." For Rupert, what else was he to do but as told and he helplessly felt the sharpness of the gravel on the lane through his socks as Bill bent down and picked up his shoes. Rupert supposed that this rough individual was going to steal his shoes and he would have to walk home without them. But, if Bill was capable of such unfeeling behaviour, what else might he be capable of? "Right," came Bill again, and standing back each time to take a run at it, he threw first one, then the other shoe high in the air over the railway cutting and all four of them, the two younger boys in total disbelief, watched them disappear from view. The wild scrub of the cutting obscured the nearside railway line and so it was not at all clear whether the shoes had fallen onto the line or had fallen into the scrub itself. "Well," said Bill, "That's that then, what d' yer think Jim?"

"I reckon so," replied Jim.

This was definitely something that Rupert desperately wanted to end. But how? Could it get worse, might they possibly be in real danger? For the moment however, there seemed to be a pause. It was a bit like the cat pausing to stare at the mouse which is not yet quite dead. The masters stared at their prey with all the satisfaction in the world written across their faces and, for the two younger boys, the suspense was becoming hard to endure.

After what seemed like an age of scrutiny from these two nasties, Bill once more came close to Rupert; so close that Rupert felt his breath on his face and it smelt bad. "Tell yer what," he said, grabbing Rupert's shirt with both hands close to his neck, "I'll get yer shoes for yer," pause, "but, if yer ever tell on uz, I'll find yer an' I'll beat yer up; OK?"

A wavering: "OK," somehow escaped from Rupert's mouth.

"OK then," said Bill and he released his prey, stood back proudly for a second or two and then ran to the fence, expertly clambered over and disappeared. He was back about a minute later and dropped Rupert's shoes on the ground in front of him. "Come on Jim, let's bugger off then," he said, and the two ruffians wandered away along the lane turning only once for a last snigger before they were gone.

The strange encounter was over. The two had not been seriously harmed, physically that is, but they had been frightened and had experienced that awful feeling of being completely at the mercy of others who may have had evil intentions. Rupert looked at the fish in the Jars and said: "You know, they are completely at *our* mercy in a way. Do you think they know how dangerous it might be for them?"

"Perhaps," said Christian, "but they have very small brains and where they live naturally is pretty dangerous anyway."

"Yes, I suppose so, but it must be fear of us which made them so difficult to catch. What must that feel like to them? Anyway, who were those boys? I'd never seen them before."

"No, nor had I."

"I can't see how they would have been part of those we saw come out of the wood because they didn't use my name like *they* did; and they seemed not to know us at all."

"That's true, but they did possibly come from the same direction."

"I wonder if they were connected with those others in some way and maybe they dared them to have a go at us?"

"Maybe."

Rupert quietened for a moment and then said: "Christian, will you tell?"

Christian also paused for a moment and then said: "Better not, I suppose."

Rugger

His Uncle Harry said he had legs like sparrow's kneecaps. This was a joke about how lanky he was. Rupert wasn't bothered about the remark; that was just Uncle Harry; he also quite often said that he must be putting horse muck in his boots to be growing so tall. Uncle Harry was a keen gardener and was married to Auntie Renie.

Mainly because of his height, just about the only sport Rupert was any good at was the high jump and he was going to be in the junior house team for sports day next term. All the kids in the junior part of the school did the scissors. The kids in the senior part of the school did the western roll and some could clear five feet. Rupert was not sure he would ever be able to do the western roll but he did not mind being in the team and he was currently the best junior high jumper in his house. His father always said that *he* had done lots of sport in his younger days and even did some boxing when he was in the army. Rupert once heard his father tell Uncle Harry that he (Rupert) was not very competitive. It was not that he minded football and cricket exactly but he was never picked for the school teams when he was at the council school. He never quite understood what it was to 'hold a straight bat'; the bat *was* straight wasn't it? Now, at the grammar school, instead of football, it was rugger and, because the ball was a funny shape, it wouldn't go where you wanted it to go if you kicked it, and so, you had to carry it instead. If you got it, you had to run with it and you were tackled for it, and you had to try to tackle somebody for it if you hadn't got it. Cricket was always played in the summer but in winter it was rugger. If you got in a tackle, you ended up rolling in the muddy grass and that was why you had to have a shower afterwards. It always seemed to Rupert to be an awful lot of bother—getting changed, then the long walk down Baxter Road to the playing field, then getting in a mess, the long walk back again and then the shower and change; and all in the space of a double period. Sometimes, in winter, instead of rugger, usually if the weather was very cold, you had to do a cross country run, when you had to run from school all the way across the fields and around the common. The girls never had to do this; just the boys and, once in the year, every year, there would be a special, house, cross country run when you earned points for your house according to where you were at the finish. This would be instead of normal lessons and all the girls, cheering and laughing, were allowed out to crowd behind the school railings to watch the finish. This first experience, in his first year here, found him quite near the back of the straggling pack, biting hard and trying to ignore this running of the gauntlet but unable to blot out: "Look, there's skinny Crownie, get a move on Crownie," from a particular female voice.

Anyway, he found it impossible to enthuse exactly when he was told he had to be in the house junior rugger team for the forth-coming inter house tournament; he thought he heard someone say: 'to make up the numbers'. "Yer goin' t' score a try then Crownie?" was now the latest taunt.

The tournament began and Priory House juniors would be playing Fosse in the first round. Rupert did not know many of the Fosse players but he had seen and heard about Geoff Shorter and knew that he not only played rugger for the junior school team but also played for the junior county team as well. Geoff was taller than Rupert as well as being much heavier looking and sort of tough looking.

Rupert resigned himself to the situation but was definitely not very comfortable about it as, directly after afternoon registration, the preparation ritual began: the changing, the trek along Baxter Road and then, with stamping feet and flailing arms to keep the circulation going to try to keep warm, the hanging about while the teachers got everybody organised. Priory won the toss and a heavily, track-suited Mr Steel, blew the whistle for the kick off. Rupert had been placed somewhere over to the right wing and managed to run up and back again, keeping more or less in line with the progress of the ball but, more importantly, managing to avoid actual contact with it. As he settled into the game, the exercise was just about keeping him warm enough and he found that perhaps it was not so bad after all and, as all situations pass eventually, it would all be over in due course. But then, all at once, the ball had become loose and, bouncing and wobbling, it was coming directly towards him. What was worse, there was nobody close enough that he could give way to. He could do no other than make a grab for it and to his, and probably everybody else's surprise he caught it dead cleanly. Now, anybody else would have begun an attack run just that split second before the actual collection. Unfortunately for Rupert, his split second allowance came afterwards instead of beforehand and, in all truth, it was more than a *split* second. In disbelief of, first of all, his great misfortune and then of his remarkable achievement, in trying to decide what to do next, he just stood there long enough to receive Geoff Shorter's shoulder full in his face.

He was walking along a road somewhere. He stumbled and nearly fell over. 'Funny place this. Where are all these kids going? They're all muddy. Ah, it's Baxter Road, we're going to the playing field for the house matches. Wait a minute, we're going the wrong way; the playing field is the other way.' Rupert closed his eyes tight for a couple of seconds and bits if his dream came back to him; 'was that Mr Steel bending over him?' He opened his eyes again. They were not going *to* the playing field, they were coming back. He closed his eyes again and shook his head. His dream was still there; he was wandering through thick tussocks of grass; there was shouting. A kid pushed past him and he opened his eyes again. He had a headache. 'Oh, drift along with the flow, but nothing seems very clear; people are chattering but I can't really hear what they are saying.'

Back in the changing room, he managed to go through the, by now, semi automatic, post games ritual and emerged into the corridor. He thought somebody had been talking to him but he was not sure. "Come on Rupert," It came again. It was Ian Crown, "Although the match took three periods instead of the usual two, we've still got History before home time."

"Oh yes," drawled Rupert. The friendly voice was reviving him and together, they wandered off towards room one.

"Get a move on you two!" was the somewhat irritated welcome from Miss Bright. "We've lost one period this afternoon and I want to get through quite a bit before the bell." The 'quite a bit' turned out to be about Theseus and the Minataur and the only other direct contact with Miss Bright, accompanied by sniggering from Maggie Driffil, was: "Really Crown R., you seem to be more dozy than usual today!"

Soon, this final trial of the day was over and he was on his way home. He had begun to realise that it was not a dream he had had; he had actually been knocked out playing that ridiculous game. He recalled seeing boxing on television when one of the boxers was knocked out. He behaved as if he were drunk; did not know where he was. That was him this afternoon. And, rather than retire him from the game, he must have gone on taking part until the end. Why was that? Did they think he was shamming? He felt that nobody really knows what you are like inside.

Crownie's neck

Rupert's first experience of hospital had been when he swallowed a lead pig. He, and the boy next to him in the waiting room, who had swallowed a threepenny bit, with respective mums, waited for the results of the x-rays and for what the duty doctor would have to say. The farmyard animal had seemed quite small in the palm of his hand but, at the age of four and a half, an oral examination of most things was quite useful backup. It was something about the taste which had made him suddenly gag strangely, and then, this enormous thing was actually stuck in his throat. Fortunately, it had been for only a second or two, although, for Rupert, a rather frightening second or two, before it was gone; and then he could not feel it at all. He could feel where it had been though and, in distress, went coughing and spluttering to his mother. The item showed up extremely clearly on the celluloid sheet, that the doctor held up to the light, and his interpretation was that, by this time, it had left the stomach and was well and truly on its way. The advice had been to let nature take its course and, three days later, just when his anxious mother was on the point of appealing again to the medical profession, the offending article emerged. For Rupert, there had been the indignity of having to use the potty for his number twos; for his mother, the daily probing and the repeated disappointment. But now, there was an outbreak of relief for him and pure joy for her. She picked it out and went to the nearest hot water tap to cleanse it; and there it was, not dull grey in patches, where the paint had chipped away but entirely bright and shiny all over.

Who can say what effect the ingestion of traces of heavy metal on the developing brain of a young boy can be, and of course, boys will be boys, but instances of irresponsible conduct would lead Rupert into various scrapes over the following years. He was entirely blameless however, (unless you believe in fairies), when one morning, just before leaving for school his mother had asked him: "Put some coal on the fire before y' go Rupert." It was Monday; there had been the weekend respite. The grammar school was only a five minute walk away at the top of the road and he would always allow just enough time; he still did not care at all for the 'dead' time before the safety of the arrival of a member of staff. In fact, he was still in the habit of waiting outside for Mrs Hood before going up into the form room. So, although the prospect of playing truant never entered his head, his apprehension of each fresh day was always there. You would have thought that this behavior would have been pretty conspicuous to discerning adults but nobody ever asked him why he was outside instead of inside with the others.

Rupert did as bidden and walked through the kitchen to the back door, opened it and stepped across the passageway to open the coalhouse door. The door opened towards him, hinged at the left hand side. As he pulled it wide, looking straight ahead, he was quite unprepared for the sound and the movement in the upper left of his vision; something was falling towards him. His reflex reaction was to jerk his head quickly away. The yard brush, which had been leaning against the inside of the coalhouse door, clattered to the floor and Rupert's head was stuck tight against his right shoulder. Any attempt to lift the head caused a stabbing pain in his neck. His crying out quickly brought his mother to the scene, and she was immediately very worried when she saw what had happened and became worse when it dawned on her that it was she who, without thinking, had pushed the yard brush onto the pile of coal and closed the door on it.

This was the time when you could get a pretty quick visit from your GP if you needed one but it was also the time when only a handful of homes had a telephone. If she went to the telephone box at the end of the road, although not far, it would mean leaving Rupert on his own. She had to think which neighbour had a telephone and decided to knock at the Prices next door. Anyway, Doctor Duggan arrived within about half an hour and soon after, the Standard Eight pulled onto the drive and his father was there too.

Doctor Duggan lightly scratched a pin across Rupert's hands and feet and asked if he could feel it; he could. "That is a good sign," he said, "but there seems to be some kind of dislocation. I should like you to take him straight away to the local hospital. Will you be able to do that?"

"Yes," said his father, looking across towards his wife who had tears in her eyes, "we can go straight away."

"I'll go back to the surgery now and phone from there to let them know you are on your way."

With Doctor Duggan gone, Rupert's father, as was his way, vented his own anxiety about what had happened in a manner which only made his wife more remorseful. "Why din't y' 'ang the brush up properly, there's a 'ook on the back o' the door?"

"I don't know, I must 'ave bin in a bit of a rush"

Seeing the distress, he said: "Well I'm sure everything'll be all right. Come on then."

At the local cottage hospital, the situation was treated with some urgency, for it was a very short time indeed before Rupert was tightly held down on a chair by one doctor while another gripped his head from behind and was firmly manipulating it back upright. Rupert winced and groaned at this severe discomfort, which seemed to go on for an eternity, but then was all over. "Now I don't want you move your head very much at all," said the manipulator, "do you understand?"

Rupert responded: "OK," but his neck felt most strangely, as though his head might topple over at any moment.

"I'm going to have a couple of x-rays taken, just to be on the safe side," and then turning to Rupert's parents: "but I'm going to admit him and keep him in traction and under observation for about a week."

This fresh news brought fresh anxiety to the faces of Rupert's parents, but they nodded their understanding. Rupert understood too; he understood that for at least a week he would be free of certain other anxieties of his own.

About an hour later, after the doctor manipulator had declared himself satisfied with the x-rays, the boy found himself flat on his back in bed, with, around his head and chin, a leather strap arrangement, which was attached to a string, which went over a pulley on the ironwork at the bed-head, and which was attached at the other end to a bag of lead shot. He was told he had to relax! He tried. It was not easy. His parents would now leave. His father needed to get back to work and his mother would need to organise what she would bring later; he still wore the standard hospital gown he had been told to change into for the x-rays and his own pyjamas would be on her list. He was in the men's ward at the front of the hospital; he was told that the children's ward was full and that anyway, they were mostly much younger than he. There were eight beds in the ward, arranged four and four opposite along the long sides of the room. His bed was the second from the door, which was at the left end of the room and faced the windows behind the beds opposite. The windows were quite high, too high to see someone walking past outside, and so there was a view of just the roofs of the houses on the opposite side of County Road and then open sky. He was not allowed a pillow and so even this view was not a comfortable one. The only completely comfortable view was in fact just the ceiling and, it was only when the pain of boredom overcame the pain of moving his head that he would take the occasional glance around. From the door, the first two beds opposite were unoccupied but then the inpatients were of varying ages, Rupert thought, though all much older than he. There was occasional conversation between the two of them to his opposite right, but the ones to his immediate right and left were very quiet and most probably sleeping. Whilst the pull on his harness was uncomfortable, it was not exactly painful provided he lay still, but, with nothing to do, time was beginning to drag; and the whole place did not seem to Rupert to be very friendly. Even the nurses seemed too busy to talk much, except to ask funny questions like: "Have you had your bowels open today?" and, to start with, Rupert was not quite sure what they meant by that.

It was after tea when his mother and father visited. He was able to change into his own pyjamas. They had also brought a carrier bag of goodies for him, spangles and a mars bar, an apple and two western adventure comic books; one was Kit Carson and the other was Buck Jones. When you get things like that, you feel a bit special and he felt reassured that he was not entirely on his own. His father showed him how he could ease forward, and then gently move back again so that the bag of lead shot would rest partly on the ironwork of the bed; and that meant that it did not pull quite so uncomfortably on his chin. He said that he should not let the nurses catch him doing it though.

Later, with his parents gone and the lights dimmed, he had placed the Kit Carson book, with a paper marker at page fifteen, on the bedside table and was just beginning to get drowsy. He became vaguely aware of voices a way off, then some banging about and voices louder; shouting even. The ward doors then opened and all in their beds were aroused and turned to see the disturbance. A female nurse led the way, followed by two male nurses who were guiding, indeed virtually carrying a very small, shouting man between them. "Come on Charlie," said one of the male nurses, "stop making this fuss. You just need to get in bed and sleep it off."

Rupert recognised Charlie. He had often seen him in the town and he had heard his parents talk of him sometimes. "'e dives off the bar for a pint," his father had said once. Rupert had seen him pick up cigarette ends from the gutter and put one in his mouth and light it. His father had said he was a dwarf and a tramp. Inside the ward, Charlie seemed to calm down immediately and the two male nurses let go of him. Then, as if at some hidden signal, he grabbed at the female nurse and shouted: "Give us a kish luv." The male nurses straight away reacted and restrained him once more but amid more shouting.

"Gaud, 'e's ad a right skin full ain't 'e," said the man in the bed to Rupert's right.

"Aye, drunk as a lord," said the man opposite.

It took something like a quarter of an hour before the nurses had the confidence to leave Charlie snoring away in his bed and very soon after that Rupert drifted away too. On waking the following morning, he looked across the room to see Charlie sitting up in bed and as bright as a button. "'ello young sir," called Charlie across to him. He had clearly 'slept off' whatever it was and for the next hour or so turned out to be the most open and friendly of the inmates. However, in an hour or so, Rupert once again looked over to an empty bed; Charlie had gone on his way and the boy had to get used to how it was obviously going to be for the rest of the week. He enjoyed his excursions through the wild west with Kit Carson and Buck Jones but, because, he had to lie flat and was constrained by his chin harness, he had to hold the book in the air over his head and, after a while it made his arms ache and he had to stop for a rest. He worked out that, if he had a frame of some sort, supporting a clear glass top, he could put the open book on top and read each page without this problem but how was he going to get this organised in just one week? He would just have to put up with it. His parents came to see him each evening and brought more goodies; he looked forward to them coming. Eventually however, even the dread of mixing with Maggie Driffil again was beginning to have more appeal than this incarceration. The experience was a contribution to the education that perhaps all awkward situations pass away sooner or later and he hoped that, maybe, a time would come when his current pre-occupation would also be a thing of the past.

A week later, the great manipulator declared that Rupert's neck had responded well and that he would be able to go home. "He must wear a neck brace during the day for another month though, just to be on the safe side," he said. "I'll show you what to do." His mother watched intently as the doctor folded some newspaper and wrapped it in a soft linen cloth to make a long rectangle. "Come here young man," he said to Rupert, and he wrapped the stiffened article around the boy's neck so tightly that he could hardly turn his head. He secured it with safety pins. "It has to be quite tight, I'm afraid," he said, "so that it gives the correct support." He smiled briefly at the boy's discomfort and added: "The time will soon pass and you'll be back to normal," and turning to his mother: "I'd like to see him just one more time, just to confirm that it will be all right to finish with the brace; say the middle of next month?"

"All right doctor, thank you. When will 'e be able t' go back t' school d' yer think?" Rupert waited in tense anticipation.

"Oh straight away; after the weekend; but no PT or games for a while; not 'til the brace comes off." This was both bad news and good news for Rupert; he could not put off facing you know who but a whole month's holiday from the subjects he most disliked.

So, back at school, and anything out of the ordinary of course aroused curiosity. There were lots of 'what 've you done?' and 'what's that 'round your neck?' until Mrs Hood made an announcement to the whole class of what had happened and that they all had to be careful not to knock or push Crown R. while he was wearing the neck brace. "Ooh er," mocked Maggie Driffil later, "we shall 'ave to be so careful, shan't we." But Rupert settled in; satisfied that he had found, for the immediate future at least, a cocoon of protection.

Mini cricket

Rupert never thought of himself as at all popular in his class, and he was no good at sports exactly, but there were some kids in his class who were not too bad towards him; enough of them to play mini cricket and he turned out to be quite good at it; now that the neck brace would be coming off within a couple of days and did not bother him so much. It was beginning to catch on also with some of the kids who were not at all friendly with him in the normal way and, when, at the next opportunity, he produced a pretty decent miniature bat and a set of miniature stumps with bails and a firm rubber ball half the size of the tennis ball, which they had used so far, he was an instant hit. "Hey, they're not bad," said Ian. And, when the other kids saw, more got drawn into playing and even an audience developed each breaktime and dinnertime when they played. Even some of the girls came to watch. He would notice Maggie Driffil, just a little way off, occasionally looking his way with what seemed to Rupert a bit of a snarl on her face. At dinnertime, his mother was surprised that, instead of having to be chased out of the house in the nick of time, he would disappear back to school directly after his meal.

It was completely in character for him to become absorbed in his latest craze; to such an extent that on one occasion, his father threatened to put the mini cricket bat on the fire if he did not pay more attention to his homework.

The craze was still going strongly three weeks later, well into the spring term, and it gave him a good deal of security because, in free time he always had enough of the right sort of kids around him. There was not so much of that dangerous idle time, when he felt so vulnerable. That was until he committed the worst sin possible. If a teacher forgot to ask for the homework to be handed in, it just was not the 'done thing' to offer a reminder. It was an art lesson with Miss Pollack at Hill View. They were involved in pencil drawing oak and chestnut twigs which Miss Pollack had distributed and nearly everyone was deeply concentrating. If anything, it was unusually quiet; was there a reason for that? Whatever it was, it was completely missed by Rupert. Before the weekend, she had set them the task of representing 'Early summer' on an eight inch by ten inch piece of white paper. He was quite proud of his watercolour of a view from the large Hill View window which looked over the woods, and which he had painted during that Saturday morning art club. It was Alan Crown who, with about just five minutes to go before the bell, whispered across: "She's forgotten about the homework."

Still missing the point and still absorbed in his pencil rendition and completely without thinking he came out with the killer line: "Do you want the homework Miss?"

"Oh, thank you Crown R. I think I had forgotten all about that." He looked up to see the faces of at least half the class glaring his way; the expressed surprise quickly turning to shear hatred. His stomach dropped. What had he done? "Would you all please put them on the end table as you go out when the bell goes."

Rupert tried to lose himself in his work again but it was not nearly as easy to concentrate as before. Surreptitiously he looked up and around and noticed Harris glaring at him. As their eyes met, Harris, with a fierce sneer, mouthed a silent: 'You prat!' and Rupert's discomfort multiplied. It was nearly time for the bell; any minute now. It was the last lesson of the morning and he would be peeling off from Smuts Lane to go home for dinner and so not going on to main school until the afternoon. Miss Pollack began organising the clearing up. Even when the bell went before everything was done, the kids knew she would still insist on everybody standing quietly before being dismissed one row at a time. Rupert was in the second row to be given the marching order but, instead of walking out of the door immediately, he feigned interest in one of the display boards; enough procrastination, he hoped, to avoid running the gauntlet outside. "Come along Crown R.," called across Miss Pollack, "I need to lock up for lunch." Rupert looked around to see that he was the last one left and he moved towards the door and went out. The short corridor of the old house, leading to the main door, was empty. He walked cautiously on and peered out; all was clear. He walked out into the bright sunshine and could only make out two or three stragglers, yards away along the bush lined drive, heading for the gateway and Smuts Lane. Taking his time, he followed on; relief returning, until that was, he was just about to pass through the gateway. Harris emerged from the bush on his right and Pongo Sieley appeared from his left.

"Right you prat," spat Sieley, "why'd you tell 'er?" and he landed a punch full into Rupert's chest.

Rupert recoiled painfully, "Ow! I dunno, I didn't think. Anyway, we'd have to hand it in sometime."

"Well, I'd forgotten mine," joined in Harris," and she's given me 'undred lines. You'd better do 'em for me or I'll beat y'up," (Where had Rupert heard that expression before?) and he followed up with his clenched fist contribution, this time, into Rupert's stomach, which made him double up; gasping for breath.

"All right," gasped Rupert trying to hold back the tears.

"And," said Sieley, delivering the killer blow, "you needn't come out on the field. You can stick yer mini cricket up yer arse!"

When Miss Pollack rounded the building, back down the drive, on her moped, starting her journey back to main school, Harris and Sieley ran off, leaving Rupert to struggle on home, tears running down his face at this almighty setback. Miss Pollack did not notice anything as she passed by and, when he went into his house, he had recovered sufficiently so that those at home did not notice anything wrong either, although his mother did notice that he was in no hurry to get back to school that day. He really tried to hide how he was inside but his father revealed that things were noticed after all when, the following

Saturday, while they were both working in the shed, he asked: "Ah yer all right Rupert?"

Rupert looked up at him, "Yes, why?"

"They tek the mick, don't they?"

It was the sudden and unexpected exposure that caused the tears, "A bit," he admitted.

"Well, kern't yer give it 'em back then?"

"Dunno," he stumbled.

"No, I suppose yer not really that way inclined are yer." and the subject was laid to rest.

And so it was. Rupert still kept his mini cricket bits and pieces with him for a while and would occasionally ask here and there if anybody wanted to play but the antagonism persisted and what interest might have remained clearly did not want to go against the grain. The craze died; just like that.

Crownie's thumb

Rupert was the elder child in his family and Ron was the youngest in his; he had two older sisters, quite a bit older, it seemed to Rupert. Ron lived not far away and, on fine Saturday afternoons or holidays, Rupert, and sometimes Peter Naylor from next door to Ron and, maybe, Brian Hobson, would find themselves at Ron's and mess about doing this and that. Rupert's bike had a parcel rack behind the seat and Ron would ride it around the flower bed in the middle of the lawn with Rupert standing on the back. He would stand, first on one leg and then on the other, then, maybe, turn around and face backwards. If they tried it the other way around, with Rupert at the pedals, he found it very difficult to keep the thing balanced because Ron was heavier than he, and he would wobble all over the place. There was also a rainwater tank on the flat roof over the passageway to their back door and the lads would climb up and play with model boats up there. It nearly always turned into a water fight and, if there was too much splashing, Ron's dad would come out and tell them to come down.

Ron had always been picked for the school football and cricket teams at the council school and he was now always picked for the junior rugger and cricket teams at the grammar school. Now that the better weather and longer evenings had arrived and with Rupert's neck fully back to normal, there would be more passing through Ron's back fence to play cricket on the grammar school field and, as likely as not, if John Boulder saw them, he would come over to join them. Ron was the best at batting. He always scored at least fifty runs. It seemed to Rupert that *he* always did most of the fielding and he was not that good at stopping the ball, particularly if it came low and fast, and so he usually ended up chasing after it. There were times, both in unofficial games like this, and also in school cricket, that he might steel himself to make a special effort but, mostly, it came to nothing and he was beginning to accept that he just did not have the killer instinct or, as his father had said, much real interest in competitive sports.

However, it was on one such occasion, with Ron and John, early evening, which gave him a considerable jolt. It was the ball coming fast and low from one of Ron's perfect strokes. It was coming straight for him and would reach him before bouncing. For no particular reason, he went for it with out of character determination, and braced himself for the sting to his hand. He was going to show them that, if only occasionally, he could pull off a great coup. He did not get it quite right though and the ball crashed awkwardly against his right thumb. He was not sure if he heard a crack but he recoiled in pain and sank to his knees; immediately shielding the injury with his other hand. It was the sheer shock and surprise which left him just kneeling there; not knowing what to do next and the other two gradually came over to him. As he removed his left hand, the three of them stared at the fleshy base of his right thumb which had already swollen to twice its normal size.

"Blimey!" said Ron.

"It's broke," said John. "That's what happens when you get a break; it swells up like that." John was in the Scouts and knew about things like this. "Do yer feel faint at all?"

"Not really, but it don't half hurt. I'd better get home." He gently cradled his injury and headed for the hole in the fence.

"We'd better pack in now," said Ron and John agreed. John headed across the school field to his house, which was diagonally opposite and Ron collected the cricket gear and trailed after Rupert.

"Y'd better go with 'im," said Ron's father to Ron, as he examined the damage, when he met them coming through the garden. "We don't want 'im flaking out on the way."

It was only five minutes before Ron delivered his charge and Rupert's father was declaring: "Y've broke it all right; 'ow on earth did it 'appen?" Rupert explained and his father replied: "We'd better get you down the 'ospital. Seems like yer gettin' a bit accident prone dun't it?" Rupert knew that this was not a question exactly and was not exactly sure what he meant by it but kind of nodded in response. "Y'll 'ave to stay 'ere wi Fran, Marge, won't yer," he said to Rupert's mother, "so I'll tek 'im just miself." He didn't seem to Rupert to be all that happy about this because it would take all of his evening.

"Well young man," said the doctor, showing them the x-ray after they had been at the hospital for a couple of hours, "you have a clean fracture of the first metacarpal. That's the long bone at the base of the thumb. We're going to have to plaster you up from your hand to nearly your elbow. You'll not be doing much with your right hand for a while. Are you right or left handed?"

Before he could answer, his father answered for him: "He's right handed all right doctor!" Rupert detected the disapproval and also detected that his father took more care with his speaking to the doctor than when he was at home.

"Well it can't be helped. He'll just have to learn to use his left much more for the next few weeks."

Rupert was eagerly anticipating how much time off this latest incapacity would earn him when the doctor went on: "Of course, he need not have any time off from school. Just needs to take care not to knock the end of the thumb which will protrude from the plaster; no PT or Games, I'm afraid until it comes off." 'What a chisel!' he thought but then at least recognised the respite once again of the PT and Games. "Well then," went on the doctor, "we'd better hand you over to Sister, although I'll still be there for a few minutes to check that the pieces are in the right place; that may hurt a bit, but it won't be for long." And, it did indeed hurt quite a bit! But, after biting very hard, it was eventually all over and he felt the bandage reinforced casing gradually go firm and tight and warm as the plaster set. The last touch was a cloth sling around his neck for him to rest this quite heavy addition to his right arm. Sister said that it would get a little bit lighter as the plaster dried out.

They got home at about ten o'clock that evening and Rupert had his first experience of getting used to dealing with this new encumbrance; like getting his shirt off and pyjama jacket on. The cast left just the tip of his thumb showing and just the top two joints of his fingers so he had some movement but, because he could not move his thumb at all, he had no significant grip. He could only hold things in his right hand if they were thin enough to be pressed against the open end of the cast by the fingers and even this was so awkward that it made them ache in no time. He was fed up and tired and decided that he would leave the problem of being able to do with his left what he had for so long taken for granted with his right until the next day.

Strangely, apart from one 'What yer done now Crownie', Rupert warmed to the fresh curiosity caused by his latest plaster regalia. That was until Maggie Driffil came up and said: "Yer a clumsy bugger, you, aren't yer! Yer alw's wearin' somethin' stupid," and then: "I bet there's nowt wrong with yer anyway, is the!" and she reached out and tapped the cast with the plastic ruler she was carrying. But, it was only a tap; perhaps she was not quite sure of herself. Whenever she came near, he could not help the same feelings of acute discomfort but, this term, somehow, he had managed to keep more or less out of her way. There had not been too many of those idle, unsupervised moments when she could prey on her favourite victim.

One person who did not seem too pleased about him was his form teacher; Mrs Hood. She did not say as much but had that look on her face that said: 'Crown R. has done it again, drawing attention to himself. Finding an excuse not to get on with his school work'. The first lesson of the day was maths with her and it was Rupert's first opportunity to try his pen in his left hand and boy, was it difficult. Not only was his writing more spidery than anything he had done before but it was almost unrecognisable. He tried using his right hand but, of course, could only get the letter and number shapes by moving his whole arm. Back to his left and, if he slowed right down, like some young child learning to write for the first time, he could produce something which looked like that but at least was legible. But, it *was* slow going! Later, when Maggie Driffil saw something he had written, she called out: "Eh up everybody, baby Crownie's now got baby writing," and her coarse laughter was echoed by some of the others.

Biology

Rupert found chemistry quite hard to understand. Some of physics was hard too, but he loved doing electricity and got twenty out of twenty for the last electricity test and only one other kid in his class got that as well. Biology was all about living things. Rupert liked anything to do with birds and animals and insects. He was particularly interested in birds and knew most of the names of the British birds in his Observer's book. Christian said that his eldest sister, who did biology in the sixth form, had told him that birds were biology but that the way they could fly was physics. Rupert could kind of understand that, because he was also very interested in aeroplanes. He was less interested in plants but the way Miss Kennington explained that all life started with plants made sense. She said that lions could only eat antelopes because antelopes ate plants and so, without plants, there would be no lions. It was not often that teachers explained things like that; usually you would do a topic like 'right angled triangles' without knowing what they were for.

Miss Kennington took them for biology in the biol. lab which was on the first floor of the main building. Christian, being a year younger, was still at the council school but his sister had taken him and Rupert into the biol. lab on the odd occasion. Christian said that the smell was from the preservative in the specimen jars in the prep. room. There were four long benches ranged one behind the other down the long room and then the teacher's bench, which was not quite as long but was wider, was on a raised platform at the front with the blackboard high on the wall behind it. You were not allowed in any of the labs without a teacher and you had to queue up outside where, as often as not, a good deal of jostling and shoving went on until the teacher arrived. Mr Berry for chemistry and Mr Hipper for physics were quite strict and made you walk in, in what they called 'an orderly fashion', and you had to sit in the same place each time where they had put you. When Miss Kennington opened *her* flood gate, a sea of black blazers burst through; usually with Maggie Driffil and Steve Crown on the crest of the leading wave and heading for the back bench. Miss Kennington's raised voice made only a marginal difference to the stampede and she settled for only a relatively lower noise level before beginning: "Settle down now 1B," and to assert her authority perhaps, as well as to separate two back row sparring partners, selected Steve Crown to give out the exercise books.

"O-ow, do I 'ave to Miss?" he drawled back.

"Yes, don't argue with me, just do as you are asked!"

"O-ow, all right," and, as soon as he let go of Maggie Driffil's wrists, she, with a smirk, took a swing at him. He ducked clear and with a broad grin at her said: "You wait 'til I get back!"

"Oo, don't hurry," she called after him as he deliberately, slowly, reluctantly made his way to the pile of books on the teacher's desk.

"Now, while that is happening," went on Miss Kennington, "I want you to listen carefully. Today, we are going to be testing for starch in a specimen of . . ." and she was stopped in mid sentence by a name called out by Steve Crown and an exercise book slicing through the air and landing in the middle of the third bench. "I said GIVE out the books, not throw them! What *do* you think you are playing at?"

"It's a long way over there."

"Oh, you're hopeless, and disrespectful; you'd better be careful!" And then: "Oh sit down; and if you can't behave properly down there, I shall have to bring you to the front. Crown I, will *you* give them out please; just put them on the end of each bench for them to be passed along." At the warning to Steve, Maggie Driffil made a mocking gesture of fear. The lesson had hardly started and already Miss Kennington was getting pretty wound up; a familiar waver developing in her voice. Ian did as bidden and she tried again: "Now, as I was saying, today we are going to be testing for starch in leaves. To do this we need to de-colourise them first of all so that they are nearly transparent. We shall then apply a staining agent which will cause any starch in the leaf to go black." Then, with voice suddenly raised: "Smith P., leave Alison alone and pay attention!" Laughter from the back row. "And, stop that laughing, it's just not funny!" There was something approaching calm as she went on: "Now, to de-colourise the leaves, we need to nearly boil them, not in water, which would wash out the starch, but in turpentine. Now, turpentine is inflammable, and so we can't heat it directly. Will you pay attention Maggie Driffil!" Pause. "We need to heat it, the turpentine, in a hot water bath, which would be one small beaker, with the turpentine, inside a larger beaker with some water. This will ensure that the turpentine does not get too hot. The apparatus is all on the side bench over there. I want you to set up tripods and Bunsen burners on heat mats; no more than three sets to each bench." There was an immediate outbreak of chattering, rustling of papers and scraping of stools. "Wait a minute, I've not quite finished yet. Sit down again." A pause for a re-establishment of calm enough, although she was now beginning to get slightly out of breath and flushed in the face. "There will be enough for two or three pupils to a set of apparatus; no more than that anywhere please. I shall come 'round to light the Bunsens and shall bring the small beakers with the turpentine and with two leaves already in each one." There was a fresh stirring. "Sit still, I've not quite finished!" Pause again. "Do not more than half fill your large beaker with water and, as soon as you think all the colour has gone, you must turn off your Bunsens and let things begin to cool down." She paused again and looked around the class, which had all the appearance of a pent up spring. "Are there any questions?"

"Can we start then miss?" called out a voice from somewhere in the middle.

"I didn't mean that sort of question, but, if you all understand what I have said, yes you . . . ." and the end of the sentence was lost in the cacophony of a world on the move.

Gradually, the slightly unruly collection of individuals achieved the near impossible and, apart from the noise level, the room seemed more or less ready for business. Miss Kennington began her round; distributing the small beakers and lighting the Bunsens but taking care to start at the front and so keep the troublesome back row clearly in view.

"Come on Miss, we want to start," called out Maggie Driffil, in mock innocence.

"You'll have to be patient." 'Miss' was just dealing with the third bench. "I'm coming to you next." And so, eventually, all fires were lit and thirty five pairs of eyes, some more enthusiastic than others, stared, each at their own personal brew. Of course, nothing happened immediately and it would take a few minutes before the water began to bubble. Miss Kennington took up position to the side and central and, slightly nervously, continuously glanced to the right and then the left like an alert radar aerial. "What's that burning smell?" she called out.

"It's Phillip Miss, 'es put 'is pencil in the flame," called back William Harris with a broad grin.

"It were an accident Miss, honest," said Phillip Smith.

"I don't believe you Smith. Don't let it happen again."

"All right Miss." And, turning to his partner: "You wait Harris, splittin' on me like that," but the continuing grins revealed the playfulness of it all.

When some teachers said things you knew they meant it but there were some, you could tell, were not like that and Miss Kennington now looked more red in the face and her hand was shaking. She called out above the noise: "While you are having to wait for a few minutes, don't waste your time; make sure your exercise book is up to date with your notes about this experiment." There was only a token response to this. "Is yours up to date Smith, and yours Harris?"

"Yes, Miss," came the reply in chorus.

"Hmm, I'll be checking in a minute. And, what about you Maggie Driffil," and then with urgent raised voice: "Take you ruler away from the flame; you've just heard me telling Smith!"

This was developing into idle time; testing time. There were twelve burning Bunsens in the room and not much was happening yet as a result. Idle time. One or two kids were beginning to stray from their places; ostensibly taking an interest in their neighbours' experiments but the opportunity for mischief was not to be lost by certain individuals. Just seconds later, it only took a minor diversion on the front bench: "Miss, our Bunsen's gone out," for 'Miss' to take her eye off the main ball and Maggie Driffil moved swiftly from her place in the far corner back row to the other end of the bench in front where Rupert and Ian were working. Rupert was not beyond mischief himself on occasion, but, at this particular point, he was actually bent over his exercise book and drawing a diagram of the apparatus. His plaster had been off for a whole week now and he was glad to be able to draw properly again; although his thumb still hurt a little sometimes. Quick as a flash, the girl grasped at Rupert's book and pulled it away. He did not see this coming and did not even have time to lift his pencil which scored a line right across the retreating page. She stood menacing in front of him; waving the book in her left hand and, hardly ever parted from it, brandishing her ruler in the other.

"Give it back," said Rupert quite nervously.

"O-oo er," said Maggie Driffil.

"What are you two up to?" called Miss Kennington; turning around to this latest disturbance.

"She's got my book!" He made a grab for it, which she easily avoided, but he was not quick enough to avoid the ruler which caught him edge on, on the back of his left hand. "Hell!," shouted Rupert in pain and he made another grab for the book. This time he got a firm hold but, as she responded once more amid the near hysterical 'Stop it!' from Miss Kennington, she misjudged her aim and instead caught the leg of the boys' tripod. The tripod tilted away and the beakers on top went with it. The liquids were clearly hot enough by now because, when they spilled, it was either the fumes from the turpentine, or maybe splashes, which caused a sheet of flame to run three quarters of the way along the bench. The other kids on the bench, and those in front scattered pretty sharply away from the spectacle; and the splashing, scolding water.

"You stupid girl!" shrieked Miss Kennington hurrying to the spot and she quickly dabbed at the flames with the nearest available article, which turned out to be Rupert's exercise book. The flames were replaced by gently rising fumes and vapour from the debris of wetted books and papers strewn about the bench top.

"Not my fault, 'e gave me a nasty look!" called back Maggie Driffil; but even she looked shocked by the experience.

"Yes, I saw 'im Miss," joined in Steve Crown; coolly exploiting the situation.

"What's that got to do with anything?" shouted Miss Kennington; tears welling up in her eyes, "this is disgusting behaviour!"

When the door opened and Mr Steel stepped in, the whole world came, at once, to a complete standstill. He shrewdly examined the young faces, all now turned towards him; mostly in surprise, some in fear, but some he perceived showing discomfort or perhaps guilt. "Is everything all right, Miss Kennington, I was just passing and thought I heard shouting?" he said calmly and deliberately.
"Yes . . . , well no, not really I suppose," she replied quietly, unable now to stop the tears.

"Why don't you go to the staff room? I'll look after these until the bell if you like."

"All right," she reluctantly answered, and looked down dolefully as though considering the offer, then slowly made her way to the door and went out.

"Right then," said Mr Steel to the class, "let's get this all cleaned up. Turn off all the Bunsen burners, empty all beakers down the sinks and put all apparatus neatly on the side bench." He walked to the end of the third bench, shaking his head at the mess and asked: "Who's experiment was this one then?"

"Ours Sir," replied Rupert.

"I might have known Crown R." His withering look made Rupert feel most uncomfortable; and he never needed to shout to deliver *his* messages.

"But, it wasn't our faul . . ."

"I'm sure you don't want me to hear your excuses do you?" interrupted the master calmly.

"No Sir." He wanted to explain but somehow Mr Steel made *him* feel guilty of something and he was quite unable to protest further. The bane of his life had spoiled his exercise book bruised the back of his hand and somehow managed to add to his less than favourable reputation; and there was nothing he could do about it.

Crescendo

It was well into the Summer of quite an eventful first school year at the grammar school. With the plaster off, the thumb felt more or less all right although Rupert could still feel a kind of familiar weakness every now and then. Doctor Duggan said this was quite to be expected for about a year but was nothing to worry about, "Just don't put unnecessary force on it for a while. It's a bit like running in a new car," and he chuckled at his own remark.

Rupert had been glad to be free of the thing although he was apprehensive because he felt it had given him more protection than just for the thumb. Now that he was once again outwardly fully able-bodied, he might also be freshly unprotected against certain other difficulties; and so it proved to be. It was as though the world had turned full circle: first lesson, maths with Mrs Hood, was over and Mr Thomas was late. Idle time, idle hands; it usually leads to mischief. He was sitting at his desk and doodling in the back of his rough book when Maggie Driffil suddenly appeared in front of him dancing weirdly. "Come on then Crownie," she taunted, "let's see yer dance then."

"Ow, get away," said Rupert but rather weakly.

"Ooo-er, get away is it? Shan't!" and as she gyrated from side to side, she reached across each time to stroke first his right cheek and then his left. Rupert had to lean back further and further to escape actual contact and lifted his right arm, to ward her off.

"Eh up lads," called out Harris, "Crownie fancies Maggie. D' yer fancy 'er then Crownie?" There was laughter from several points around the room and Maggie Driffil grinned delightedly to her audience over her shoulder and then returned to her prey. Rupert leaned back just a little too far and, despite trying to save himself, with both arms flailing, and amid an outcry of hooting laughter, he toppled backwards in a heap on the floor. Quick as a flash, Maggie Driffil lifted Rupert's desk lid, grabbed a handful of whatever she could reach from inside and tossed such towards the open classroom doorway. Rupert, momentarily confused as to whether to save himself or his property, rolled over and quickly crawled on all fours towards the doorway. Pongo Sieley was leaning against the open door and, with some gentle footwork 'helped' a couple of Rupert's textbooks, which had landed within reach, out into the corridor. He also managed to kick Rupert's leg as he went past to retrieve them. Maggie Driffil, on seeing Rupert sprawling across the floor, ran through the doorway and launched herself on top of him and grabbed his hair with both hands. Rupert was becoming quite distraught; this was the worst onslaught yet. She was pulling at his hair and pulling his head back as she sat across his back. "Ride 'im cowboy," yelled Harris.

"Yippee!" yelled Maggie Driffil and then: "Ooo-ff," as somehow Rupert had managed to elbow her in the side and dislodge her. She rolled off and, as Rupert turned around to her he found her sitting on the floor with her back to him. What happened next was all so quick and, afterwards, he did not know how he managed to do what he did, but in sheer desperation, frenzy, semi-consciousness, exhaustion maybe, he flailed his right hand, edge-wise and caught her hard on the right cheekbone. It was not a punch, which would almost certainly have put his hand and arm back in plaster, it was more a karate chop although, heavens knows, such would not, deliberately, have been in Rupert Crown's repertoire. The blow was so strong that she fell sideways and banged her head on the floor; thereby receiving two blows for the price of one. She recovered immediately and stood up, face already reddening, to find herself looking straight into the face of a furious Mr Thomas; with all the noise, this time, nobody had heard his approaching footsteps. All those who had crowded around the door to see the sport, on seeing their teacher appear, had scurried back inside and even Sieley was quick enough to pass himself off as an innocent spectator and he slinked away. It was difficult to tell which of the remaining combatants was the more disorientated but as Rupert cottoned on to why it had suddenly gone quiet, he also struggled to his feet and the two of them faced justice.

"This is totally unacceptable behaviour when I am unavoidably delayed," he delivered calmly. It was strange how such a calm voice held so much more power than a, probably, expected yell. "Can you think of any reason why I should not take you both straight to the headmaster?"

There was a shocked silence for a second before first Rupert and then Maggie Driffil uttered a plaintive: "No sir."

Rupert was trembling and mentally preparing himself for the worst. He did not know who he feared the more; the Headmaster or Maggie Driffil and what she may try to do about this when she next had her chance. He did not look at his antagonist but she also was in a very flustered condition. "Well then," went on Mr Thomas, "let's see what we do about this. Whose things are these on the floor?"

"They're mine sir," uttered Rupert, trying hard to get himself together.

"Well get them picked up then. Don't make any plans for going home at four o'clock tonight. You'll both come to my detention tonight in room five and you'll be lucky if you get away before five!" This was something like a reprieve, Rupert thought with great relief. He was unstreetwise and naïve in many ways but later it did occur to him that it was such a strange turn around that maybe Mr Thomas did not want to explain to the headmaster why he was so late getting to his lesson.

So, at the end of school, Rupert was first to report to room five. "Sit over there, by the window Crown," and, as Maggie Driffil came in: "and you, Miss Maggie, can sit over the other side by the wall. And, you are not going to waste your time." He handed them each a text book and some sheets of lined paper. "Turn to page twenty four and I want you to, **neatly** (heavily emphasising the word), copy out the section on The Midlands Coalfields, including the diagrams. **If** (more heavy emphasis) you finish before five o'clock, I may let you go *if* your work is of sufficiently good quality. Is that all clear?"

"Yes sir," came back the half muted chorus and they proceeded with their tasks. There were three other kids spread around the rest of the room and they too were given some text book work to do. Rupert kept his head well down; not at all wishing to make eye contact with his arch enemy on the other side of the room.

Mr Thomas let the other three go at about half past four; presumably they had committed lighter sins. As five o'clock approached The Midlands Coalfields remained stubbornly uncopied completely but Mr Thomas, maybe not wishing to be in detention himself beyond this, called across to Maggie Driffil: "All right then Miss Maggie, let me see what you've done." She stood up, collected the papers and the book and wandered over to the teacher's desk. "Hmm," he uttered, as he shuffled through the papers, I suppose this will have to do. All right then. Now, I don't ever want to see behaviour like that again, is that clear young lady?"

"Yes sir," she said. Rupert thought that 'lady' was stretching things a bit far in her case but he still kept his head well down.

"All right then, off you go," and she turned and went out. "Now Crown, let me see yours." Since Rupert was sitting right in front of the teacher's desk, he just handed his papers over. "The writing's a bit spidery Crown, isn't it?"

"Yes sir, it's my thumb. I'm not used to using it again yet and after a while it sometimes still aches."

"Hmm, well, ye-es. I suppose so. All right then," and he inclined his head towards the door. "But, remember what I have said to both of you, OK?"

"Yes Sir," and Rupert, too, moved towards the door but hoping that there had been sufficient time for Maggie Driffil to be well clear. Craning his neck first, to check the emptiness both ways, he moved into the corridor. Room five was located about half way along it. He turned right and headed for the next main corridor; the one leading to the main outside door and peered cautiously around before continuing. It seemed strange to have these vast arteries entirely to himself. Although early summer, the sky was overcast with low dark cloud and, when he opened the door, he was bathed in a swirling cold draught as he pushed on outside. All was quiet here too; not a soul around. Confidence building, he walked steadily along the outside of the building towards the quadrangle by the new block; his classroom block. There were two main gates along the Smuts Lane side and, after crossing the quad, he would be going to the nearest one and turning left towards Meadow Road and the security of home. The other gate would be used by anyone heading towards the centre of town. As he turned the last corner into the open space before the gates, he saw a girl just about to go through the far one. It was Maggie Driffil. He was surprised that she was such a short distance ahead of him. Had she been waiting for him? Or, perhaps she had slipped into the block to get something on her way past. It was pretty quiet, no traffic at all on Smuts Lane, so, she may have heard his footsteps, or she may have looked over her shoulder anyway, incidentally. When she noticed him, the thirty yards or so away, she stopped and turned. Rupert stopped also.

"You've 'ad it now Crownie," she called across venomously. "Just you wait 'til tomorrow," and she went off. Rupert's stomach dropped and his hand began to shake as he went out onto the lane. He stood and watched her go; thankfully putting an increasing distance between them. She turned again and, yelling, this time: "Just you wait."

Come the dawn

Rupert was just about composed again when he walked in through the back door. "Yer a bit late Rupert," was his mother's greeting, "where yer bin?"

"Owh, just playing on the field."

"Well, yer might let me know if yer goin' t' be late 'ome; so's I don't worry about where y'are. "Ave yer got any 'omework? You know what yer dad ses; y've got t' do it before yer do anything else."

"Yes, I've got some maths to do," he answered resignedly.

"Well get on with it then because I shall need the table soon."

He let out a sadly stretched: "Okaaay" and then began to 'get on with it'. He found it difficult to concentrate on working out the values of 'y' for various values of 'x' in the formula 'y = x^2 + 3x +1' and when he came to draw the graph, it had a funny kink in the curve which he wondered perhaps should not be there. He kept straying to watch his sister, Fran, playing on the floor with a row of her 'dollies'. Anyway, under the circumstances, he felt he had made a reasonable attempt at it and declared to his mother that the table was now free. He wandered down the garden to the shed and hacked idly at a piece of wood with a chisel but there was nothing particular he wanted to make and, anyway, the light was fading so he went back to the house. His father arrived home and everybody settled down to watch the television. Some of the kids at school had said that they would be watching 'Son of Fred' with Spike Milligan that evening. He asked his dad if he could watch it but his dad said it was on too late and 'it were rubbish anyway'.

So, just a little while after Fran, he was in bed too. But, what a terribly long night. Every time he closed his eyes and tried to drift away, the menacing face of the devil glared straight at him. He knew he had better not put on his room light because, if his dad saw it, it would make him cross but, he found his torch under the bed and tried to read a bit more of Treasure Island under the bedclothes. The trouble was that, five pages later, he had absolutely no recollection of what they had been about. He turned back to read them again but very soon after that, what had been a reasonable, white light from the torch, was now a distinctly duller yellow verging on orange; the battery was running down. He was lying there; exhausted but wide awake and, like a condemned man, was helplessly awaiting his fate. Nothing he could do about it. It had been bad enough waiting for his parents to return from the parents' evening, the week before, because he was pretty certain he would get a bad report from Mr Thomas but, when they came home, the disaster quickly unfolded: just about all of the reports were very bad indeed! They had grilled him to a cinder. It did not matter about 'late to bed' that night; he had to endure the post mortem, fine detail by fine detail. "We were so ashamed," said his mother, "and Mrs Robson, across the road, come up to us and sed 'ow Valerie were doin' ever s' well, and asked 'ow you were doin'. Owh dear; I dunno."

"What about Mr Bearford for metalwork and Miss Pollack for art?" Rupert had wailed; tears streaming down his face.

"That's only two of 'em," returned his dad, "what about yer Maths and yer Science and yer English and yer History and Geography and French and

Latin? There's going to 'ave to be some changes Rupert!"

And here now, he was in another scrape, the utter torture of the waiting and fearing the worst. Where was the escape from all this pressure? He left it as late as he possibly could before leaving for school the next day. He had a funny feeling in his stomach and a bit of a headache. He supposed that he had slept eventually, during the night, but it could not have been for very long. He thought it must be very close to the bell as he went through the gate and onto the quad. He went over to the tennis practice wall, which was opposite the classroom block and leaned back; looking out for Mrs Hood's approach. Harris came sauntering across the quad and noticed Rupert. "What yer waitin' there for Crownie? A yer scared o' somat?" With every fresh indicator, Rupert's discomfort rose to a new level and Harris called across as he approached the block: "She ain't 'arf mad. Y'ain't 'arf in fer it."

Mrs Hood appeared and Rupert reacted swiftly going inside just a couple of seconds ahead of her. As she dealt with registration, Rupert tentatively stole a glance across the room. Maggie Driffil was sitting quietly and looking straight forward. He had expected eyeball contact and a menacing expression but no; nothing, how strange. Mrs Hood came to the end of the early morning preparations and left the room. They were all due in the physics lab for first lesson today and followed her: down the stairs, out and across the quad to the main building. Rupert had sprung to his feet quickly and was keeping up to within a few feet of her, just to be safe. He had no idea what secret evil Maggie Driffil might wield. But there really appeared to be nothing. In the afternoon, she passed by in one of the corridors, on the way to History, and, nothing. She did not acknowledge him in any way at all.

And so it was, the next day, and the next week too. It was over. Just like other bad things he had experienced, if you bit hard, sooner or later, it would be over. As Rupert became used to his release from torment, he came home from school one day to hear that it was also all over for Auntie Ada.